Goat and Big Mean

by Liza Charlesworth

Big Mean Toad's Boat

ISBN: 978-1-338-84446-7

Art Director: Tannaz Fassihi; Designer: Cynthia Ng; Illustrated by Michael Robertson
Copyright © Liza Charlesworth. All rights reserved. Published by Scholastic Inc.

3 4 5 6   68   26 25 24

Printed in Jiaxing, China. First printing, June 2022.

SCHOLASTIC

It is Goat.
"I want to roam on the road.
But I see a moat," says Goat.

"A boat can float on
a moat," says Goat.
"But I see Big Mean Toad!"

3

"Can I get on your boat?"
says Goat.
"Nope!" croaks Big Mean Toad.

Goat says, "If I get a ride,
you can get a red coat."
"Nope!" croaks Big Mean Toad.

Goat says, "If I get a ride,
you can get a fine soap."
"Nope!" croaks Big Mean Toad.

6

Goat says, "If I get a ride,
you can get a load of oats."
"Nope!" croaks Big Mean Toad.

Goat says, "If I get a ride, you can roam on the road with a nice, nice goat." "OK!" croaks Big Mean Toad.

Big Mean Toad's Boat

Goat and Big Mean Toad
float on the moat in the boat.
It is fun!

Goat and Big Mean Toad
roam on the road.
It is fun!

Did Toad like Goat? Yup!
Did Goat like Toad? Yup!

Then Goat says,
"Can I change your name
to Big Nice Toad?"

"Yup!" croaks Big Nice Toad.
"It is a fine, fine name."

Read & Review

Invite your learner to point to each *oa* word and read it aloud.

boat

load

oats

croaks

soap

road

float

moat

coat

goat

toad

roam

Fun Fill-Ins

Read the sentences aloud, inviting your learner to complete them using the *oa* words in the box.

> moat Goat boat coat road

1. Goat wants to go across the _____.

2. Big Mean Toad has a _____.

3. Big Mean Toad does not want soap or a _____.

4. Big Mean Toad DOES want to roam on the _____.

5. At the end, Toad becomes pals with _____.